THE GREATEST ADVENTURES IN THE WORLD

William Tell

AND THE
APPLE FOR FREEDOM

TONY BRADMAN & TONY ROSS

ORCHA

ORCHARD BOOKS

The text was first published in Great Britain in a gift collection called
The Orchard Book of Swords, Sorcerers and Superheroes with full colour illustrations by
Tony Ross, in 2003
This edition first published in hardback in 2004
First paperback publication in 2005

3 5 7 9 10 8 6 4 2

Text © Tony Bradman 2003
Illustrations © Tony Ross 2004

The moral rights of the author and illustrator have been asserted.
All characters and events in this publication, other than those clearly in the public domain,
are fictitious and any resemblance to real persons, living or dead, is purely coincidental.

All rights reserved.
No part of this publication may be reproduced, stored in a retrieval system, or transmitted,
in any form or by any means, without the prior permission in writing of the publisher,
nor be otherwise circulated in any form of binding or cover other than that in which it is
published and without a similar condition including this condition being imposed on the
subsequent purchaser.

A CIP catalogue record for this book is available from the British Library.

ISBN 978 1 84362 476 9

Printed and bound in Germany by GGP Media GmbH, Poessneck

The paper and board used in this book are made from wood from responsible sources

Orchard Books
An imprint of Hachette Children's Group
Part of The Watts Publishing Group Limited
Carmelite House, 50 Victoria Embankment, London EC4Y 0DZ

An Hachette UK Company
www.hachette.co.uk
www.hachettechildrens.co.uk

CONTENTS

CHAPTER ONE
GOVERNOR GESSLER

WILLIAM TELL WAS A HUNTER who lived long ago in the Swiss Alps. He was a wonderful husband and father, a terrific mountaineer, and the best shot with a crossbow in Switzerland – in short, a good man respected by his friends

5

and neighbours. And all Tell wanted was a happy, quiet life with his family.

Unfortunately for him, he'd picked the wrong time and place to be born.

In those days, the Austrian emperor ruled Switzerland, and his mail-clad soldiers terrorised the Swiss people. They protected the emperor's tax-gatherers, who stripped the people of almost everything they had. And those who protested were put in prison, or hanged – their families too, sometimes.

Of course, like the rest of the Swiss people, Tell hated the tax-gatherers, and some of the things he'd seen the Austrian soldiers doing made him angry. But he wasn't going to put his family at risk. So, hard as it was for him, Tell kept his feelings to himself, and always did his best to stay out of trouble.

And that's how things might have stayed – if it hadn't been for Gessler.

"Who is this Gessler, anyway?" Tell asked a neighbour one day. Tell had been hunting up in the mountains for a couple of weeks, and since he had been back in his home village, he had heard the name Gessler mentioned more than once.

"The new governor, just arrived from Austria," the neighbour whispered, glancing over his shoulder. "He's a friend of the emperor, and he's very cruel. He threw a farmer out of his house and took it for himself, he's doubled everybody's taxes, and no one knows what he'll do next…"

Tell said nothing – but he didn't like the sound of this Gessler at all.

CHAPTER TWO

THE NEW RULE

A FEW DAYS LATER, TELL decided to go to Altdorf, the nearest town, to buy some provisions. His youngest son, Walter, asked if he could come, and Tell said he could. They set off early, Tell with his crossbow slung over his back, and a quiver full of deadly bolts hanging from his belt. When he'd said goodbye to his wife and other sons, he had promised that they would be home by dusk.

It was a lovely spring morning, and Tell enjoyed walking with his son through the Alpine forests and meadows. But when they arrived in Altdorf, Tell soon felt uneasy. There were dozens of Austrian soldiers in the streets, and the Swiss people who were out hurried along, their heads down.

"Why does everyone look so worried, Father?" Walter asked.

"I don't know," said Tell. "But I don't think we'll stay long…"

They went into the market square, where Tell always bought the family's provisions. The stalls were there as usual, but both buyers and sellers were quiet, subdued. Tell and Walter headed for the first stall they wanted, but to get to it they had to pass through an open space in the heart of the square.

A tall pole stood at the centre of the space, and perched on top of it was a man's hat – a big, expensive-looking hat decorated with peacock feathers.

A couple of Austrian soldiers were standing by the pole, leaning on their pikes and talking to each other, watching Tell and Walter as they approached.

Tell thought it was odd for there to be a hat on a pole in the middle of the market square…but he just shrugged, and decided to ignore it.

He took Walter's
hand, and they kept
right on walking.
Suddenly
the soldiers
shouted, and
came running
after them.
Tell stopped
and turned,
making
sure that
his son
was behind
him. Walter
peeked
at the
soldiers.

They stood glaring at Tell, their pikes lowered and pointing at him.

"You know the new rule," snarled one of them. "And you'd better obey it pretty sharpish, too, my man, or you'll find yourself in serious trouble."

"New rule?" said Tell, puzzled. "I'm sorry, I've been away for a while."

Tell could see that a large crowd was beginning to gather. More soldiers arriving, and the buyers and sellers from the market watching the scene closely.

"Very well, I'll explain it," the soldier said slowly, as if Tell were stupid. "Everyone who passes through the square has to bow to the governor's hat."

"The new governor thinks you Swiss peasants need to be taught a lesson," said the other soldier. "Even his hat is more important than any of you!"

Tell looked up at the hat perched on the pole, then returned his gaze to the soldiers. They grinned at each other, and then at him. Tell frowned. He knew his safest move would be to obey their rule. But he also knew the rule was meant to humiliate the Swiss people, to make them feel they were nothing.

He understood now why everyone in Altdorf looked cowed and beaten. This was the last straw, Tell thought. The Austrians had gone too far.

"So what are you waiting for?" said the first soldier. "Let's see you bow."

"I can't do that," Tell said quietly, his voice steady. "No – I won't do that."

The crowd murmured in surprise, and the grins instantly vanished from the soldiers' faces. They blustered, and shook their pikes at Tell, and tried to make him do what they said. But Tell just stood there in front of them, his arms folded and his face set, staring them down with his steely blue eyes.

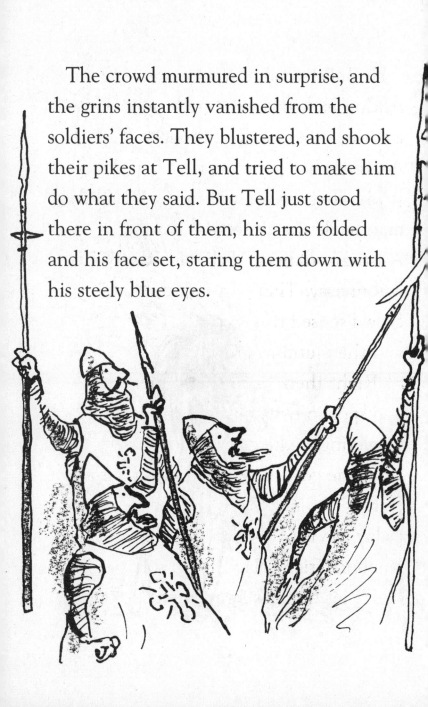

And if the
truth was
known, this
impressive,
strong-looking
man made the
Austrian soldiers
feel uneasy. The
crowd sensed this,
and the murmurs grew.

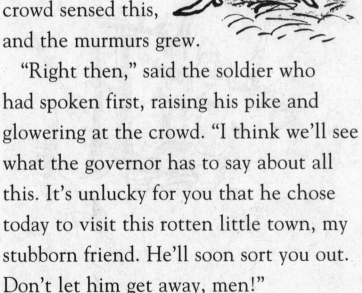

"Right then," said the soldier who
had spoken first, raising his pike and
glowering at the crowd. "I think we'll see
what the governor has to say about all
this. It's unlucky for you that he chose
today to visit this rotten little town, my
stubborn friend. He'll soon sort you out.
Don't let him get away, men!"

The soldier marched off into a large tavern on one side of the square. Several other soldiers moved forward to guard Tell, while the rest formed a cordon round the square, facing the crowd, pikes lowered. A few moments later, the first soldier emerged from the tavern, followed by another man.

CHAPTER THREE

GESSLER'S CHALLENGE

TELL KNEW IMMEDIATELY THAT the man following the soldier was Gessler. The governor was tall and fleshy, had a mean, arrogant face, and wore rich clothes and lots of golden chains and rings. Gessler kept his cold eyes fixed on

Tell as he crossed the square. He stopped in front of Tell, who noticed Gessler had a napkin in one hand, an apple in the other.

"I hate having my lunch interrupted," Gessler said, scowling. "It does terrible things to my digestion…now, why won't you bow to my hat?"

"I just won't, that's all," said Tell, and scowled back at the Austrian.

"Well, we can't have that, can we?" said Gessler. Then he turned to the soldier who had fetched him. "You know what to do, man," Gessler snapped. "Arrest him, and don't bother me again. He's only a stupid, ignorant Swiss peasant – and I've got far more important things on my plate, ha ha!"

Gessler started walking away towards the tavern, laughing at his own joke and holding his napkin over his nose. Tell tensed, and several of the soldiers moved forward nervously to do as Gessler had ordered, the crowd muttering. But just then Walter jumped out from behind his father.

"My father's not stupid, and he's not a peasant!" he yelled. "He's William Tell, a great hunter and the best shot with a crossbow in all of Switzerland!"

"Is that so?" said Gessler, stopping in his tracks. He came back to stand in front of Tell, looked him up and down. "Are you really such a good shot?"

"Yes, he is!" shouted someone in the crowd. "And you should let him go!"

"Perhaps I will," said Gessler. "If he shows me what he can do…"

Gessler paused and tossed the apple he was holding to Tell. "Could you hit that at a hundred paces?" he said, smiling. "You'll leave here a free man if you can."

"I could," said Tell, and tossed the apple straight back to Gessler. "You're very confident," murmured Gessler, still smiling. "So maybe we'd better make it a little more difficult for you. We need something to rest the apple on, but what? I know! How about somebody's head?"

Then Gessler's smile vanished, and he stared at Tell. "Your son's, for example?" he said.

The crowd gasped again. Tell reached out and pulled Walter to him.

"No, it's far too risky," he said. "I refuse to put my son in danger."

"Ah, but you already have," said Gessler, his voice silky smooth now. He was obviously enjoying himself. "Your choice is simple, Tell. Make the shot – or I'll have your son put to death right here. What do you say?"

The crowd fell silent now, shocked by Gessler's threat. Tell wondered if he and Walter could get away. But there were too many soldiers, and Tell realised it would be impossible.

He raged inside, told himself he'd been a fool to come to Altdorf today, and a bigger fool not to bow to the hat. But then Walter spoke, his voice suddenly breaking into Tell's thoughts. "You can do it, Father," said Walter, taking Tell's hand. "I know you can."

Tell looked into his young son's eyes and saw the trust there, the unshakeable belief that his father could make this difficult shot and save their lives. Walter wasn't afraid – and Tell knew he couldn't let him down.

So Tell nodded at Gessler, let go of Walter, and unslung his crossbow.

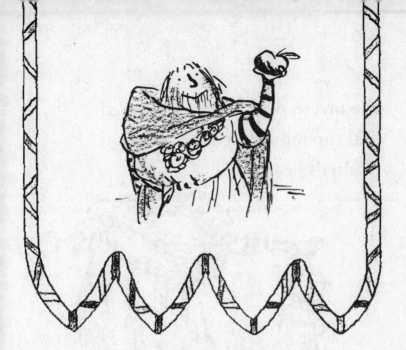

CHAPTER FOUR

AN APPLE AND
AN ARROW

"PUT THE BOY IN FRONT OF the tavern door," said Gessler, still smiling, not taking his eyes off Tell for a second. "That's near enough a hundred paces."

A couple of the soldiers took Walter to

the tavern door. Gessler followed,
and carefully placed the apple on
Walter's head.

Then Gessler walked back to Tell,
the crowd watching them silently from
beyond the soldiers' pikes.

"Well, then," said Gessler, standing
close to Tell, whispering in his ear. "This
is it, your moment of truth. Fire whenever
you're ready…peasant."

Gessler stood to the side, smirking. Tell looked at him, then took two bolts from his quiver. He fitted one in the crossbow, and slipped the other into his belt where he could get to it more quickly. He raised the crossbow – and paused.

Tell looked along the bolt and over the cobbles in front of him. The world narrowed to the small figure of Walter in the distance, and the even smaller green dot on his son's head. A blood-filled image of what would happen if he fired too low popped into Tell's mind, and he quickly pushed it out again.

Walter smiled at his father. Tell took
a deep breath, held it, aimed. Then he
breathed out slowly, squeezing the trigger
as he did so. Suddenly the crossbow's
string twanged, the sound loud in the
hush, and the bolt flew towards Walter,
a deadly blur followed by every pair of
eyes in the square.

The bolt THWACKED into the tavern door, the apple exploding in a shower of green and white pieces, and Walter raised his arms in triumph.

The crowd exploded too, yelling, cheering, calling out Tell's name. They moved forwards, the soldiers looking even more uneasy and backing off all the while.

Walter ran to his father, and Tell fell to his knees to hug his son.

"Very touching," sneered Gessler, his smirk gone. "And I suppose it was good  shooting. But one thing puzzles me, Tell. Why did you take two bolts?"

"The second was for you, Gessler, if anything had gone wrong," said Tell, angry, but deeply relieved. He rose to his feet. "Come on, Walter, let's go—"

"Not so fast, Tell!" snapped Gessler. "You heard him, men! He's just admitted he wanted to assassinate me, the emperor's governor! Arrest him!"

If the crowd had been angry before, Gessler's words simply helped to make them furious. There were catcalls and boos and suddenly things were being thrown at the Austrians – cabbages and eggs and clods of earth, even cobbles. The soldiers pushed back at the crowd, and Tell saw his chance.

"Run, Walter!" he yelled, "Into the crowd – they'll take care of you!"

Walter didn't need to be told twice. He ducked past the soldiers advancing on his father, and dived through the legs of those facing the crowd. At the same time Tell jumped on to the nearest market stall, quickly fitting the second bolt into his crossbow. He levelled it at the soldiers, who stopped.

"You've just signed your own death warrant, and that of your family," Gessler snarled, his eyes full of hate. "You won't get out of this square alive, and so long as there is breath in my body, it will be my mission to make sure your whole family is tracked down and killed. I'll do it, believe me I will."

"Oh, I believe you, Gessler," said Tell, swinging his crossbow in the governor's direction. "And that's why you leave me with no choice."

Tell pulled the trigger for a second time that morning, and the bolt flew straight into the Austrian governor's evil heart. Gessler slumped to the ground and died instantly.

The crowd fell silent again for a brief moment, and the soldiers stood looking shocked and confused. Then the crowd roared and surged forward like a great beast, sweeping the hated soldiers away.

A few seconds later, the pole
– and Gessler's hat – came
crashing down. By the
end of that morning
there wasn't a single
Austrian soldier left
in Altdorf. The
people had sent
them all packing,
and revelled in their
freedom. Tell had
found Walter safe
and unharmed, but
the people wouldn't
let them go home.
They carried Tell and
his son round on their
shoulders, cheering.

Eventually, they put Tell on a market stall, and he spoke to them.

"I learned something today," said Tell, his strong voice filling the whole square. "I wanted a safe, happy life for my family, but there's only one way to make sure of that. We've brought freedom to one Swiss town – now we have to bring it to the whole of Switzerland. Down with the Austrians!"

The crowd roared again, and soon messengers were hurrying to villages and towns all over Switzerland. It was the beginning of a war of liberation. As Tell stood in the market square of Altdorf with his arm round Walter, he knew there were difficult times ahead. But there was no going back now.

The Swiss people did eventually free themselves from the Austrians, and William Tell played a leading part in the long struggle. He is remembered to this day as a hero in Switzerland, and all around the world – a simple, honest man who loved his family, and who was finally pushed too far by a tyrant.

And he is remembered as the man who shot an apple for his country's freedom.

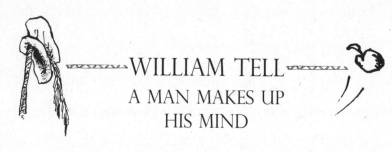

WILLIAM TELL
A MAN MAKES UP
HIS MIND

BY TONY BRADMAN

As with so many legendary figures, nobody knows if William Tell really existed. The name first appears in the fourteenth century, in stories about the Swiss people's struggle for freedom from the Austrian empire. The stories quickly became popular, and in the centuries since, the legend of William Tell has been told over and over again – in books, films, on TV, even in an opera!

William Tell has many similarities to England's Robin Hood. Tell is a great archer and a good man, and eventually takes the lead in a fight against evil oppressors. But he differs from Robin Hood in several ways too. He's a family man, for a start, with a wife and children, a great hunter respected by his friends and neighbours. And he's also reluctant to get involved in the conflict with the Austrians – he doesn't want to put his family at risk.

But that's where another common element of folk tale and legend comes in – Fate. In all the stories about William Tell we see that he's a good man. He loves his family, and he loves his country. And the Austrians are definitely pretty evil – they've invaded Switzerland, and they're busily oppressing everyone. Gessler, in particular, is a very nasty piece of work and needs to be stopped.

So when William Tell takes his son into town and walks past the pole with the hat on it, we have the feeling that his meeting with Gessler was always destined to happen. We get much the same feeling when the young Arthur pulls the sword from the stone and a great British legend begins. Neither character seems to seek their heroic role. Instead it finds them.

William Tell still has to make his mind up to go along with his Fate. But he does just that. He chooses freedom, whatever the cost, therefore fulfilling his destiny. And there's a sense of rightness about that – rather like an arrow hitting its target!

THE GREATEST ADVENTURES IN THE WORLD

TONY BRADMAN & TONY ROSS